The Oceans In Seashells

S

Morning Waves

Her lips smiled and
    eyes closed tightly as
    the morning waves repeatedly
    lapped at her feet
Sea foam crawling between her toes
    asking her to remember his tongue
    doing the same merely hours ago
The water covering her feet and making them wet
    but without the same soul
    that mouth of his had

The ocean could cover her of course

But the sea on its roughest days couldn't compare
    to how she swore that she was drowning
    in the fluid she forced from him
Only to be brought above the surface again
    when his lips met hers and they shared
    the salty taste of sex that
    seawater was always jealous of

A Piece of Summer

The summer sun felt so sweet on her soft skin
     as she picked and collected flowers topless
Taking in the light of our nearest star
     and growing towards it
The same way plants did as she
     gathered their jewels
A stray bumblebee or two would stop by
     as she held out a bloom for their plump
     little bodies to dive into
     and collect their quota of nectar and pollen
     before buzzing away busily
She loved the summer and just wanted to bring
     a tiny piece of it back
     to brighten her home

Mundane

The mundane morning routine on a day
    that was like any other
After brushing my teeth
    I turned and
    opened the bedroom door

There she was

Standing in my shirt
    and nothing else
She dropped to her knees and informed me
    that I wasn't going to work today

Remote

The movie played while her head rested
      on his lap
Her wandering hands couldn't keep themselves
      from finding their way through a zipper and
      massaging the soft skin of his cock
She smiled and almost giggled to herself when
      he started getting hard in her hand
That was when he chuckled and told her that
      he knew the remote wasn't in there

A Good Dream

With a warm coffee mug in hand
      socked feet stepped across the floor
      past the kitchen island and
      back into the bedroom

He was still sleeping
      naked under the sheets
      and
      apparently
      having a good dream

She took another sip and watched the
      rise in the sheets
      twitch and move slightly from whatever
      might be happening on the other side
      of his dreaming eyes
Fantasies of her own ran through her
      imagination for countless moments
      until she decided to set the coffee down
      on the dresser

Fingers wrapped around the thin sheets covering his
      thick
      heavy
      cock

She slowly stroked him and watched
       sleepy eyes open
Continuing to move her hand up and down
       on the flesh wrapped in linen
       until he groaned and gave a reason
       to wash them

Candle

From room to room she walked with
      a single flame to light her path
She held the candle with both hands
Letting the hot wax
      drip
      fall and
      collect on her fingers
The sight of the hardened wax saddened her
How she wished he was there to provide
      the comfort and warmth that came
      when he did in her hands

Faithless

I had been faithless for so many years
        but with pure divinity on her knees before me
        I felt new
Hands folded themselves
        around my flesh in prayer
She spoke holy words against my skin
        in an effort to save my soul
Determined to pull the name of God
        from my lips

And she did

She made me believe

Eulogy

Skin was roused as the sun set
    and darkness descended upon the room
Hands blindly found their way
    from her throat to where
    they could explore the depths of her flesh
Heavy exhales gave way to a sweet voice that
    whimpered as her body
    succumbed to his touch
Sounds that were deciphered by his ears
    as a eulogy to the light

Filthy

Come closer
Let me hold your cheek to mine
    while I whisper my wishes
    for your filthy little mind to hear

Shadows and Light

She was lovely
Knees and elbows on sofa cushions
    and a backside high in the air
Her skin entangled in the silent struggle
    between shadows and light
       as each tried to claim her soft skin as their own

I just stood there

Watching her breathe

Wanting so badly to touch her but nervous
Afraid that if I did
    it would be like a painter trying to add
       new details to a centuries old work of art
Spoiling something that was already a classic

Living Room Floor

They couldn't wait and she dropped to her
       hands and knees
He fucked her hard on the
       living room floor as
       rain poured from the sky
His hands reached up for her throat
       as he poured into her
There was no lightning
       but it didn't matter
They'd brought their own thunder

Red Lips

Let those red lips show these fingers
what you're going to do to me

Mmmm...

Good girl

So Fucking Good

I saw eyes close softly before watching her
     smile
     swallow and
     open wide to show me

How could I not kneel next to her and
     use my tongue to dig into the mouth
     that had just made me feel so fucking good?

And my God
     the taste of those kisses

Breached

Masculine arms were wrapped around her body
        from neck to navel
Like the thickest blanket on a winter's night
        after the fire had gone cold

That left hand of his dropping

Fingertips digging under elastic

He found and cupped her
        before simply holding her open while lips
        feasted on earlobes and the skin on the back
        of her neck
Teeth sunk into her flesh while a strong hand
        firmly held her throat

She rocked back and forth

Begging for something to be inside of her
But he held her open and apart for so long
        she nearly shed a tear when an assertive finger
        finally breached the entrance of her body

Getting Home

She lay face down on the mattress
Smiling before lifting her ass and taking a photo
     to send while he was at work
The ache he felt throughout the rest of his day
     was torture
All he could think about for hours was
     getting home to fuck her there

Locked Eyes

Foreheads held together
Eyes locked in a gaze
Breaths that wrapped around each other before
       disappearing into the air
Her hand dropped down his chest
       past his waist and
       folded around him
His flesh was soft as she squeezed him
       between her fingers before
       slowly pulling and
       gently twisting

"Don't look away."

She spoke with a focus in her eyes that
       demanded attention
He grew longer and harder in her hand
A transformation she loved to feel while he
       fought to maintain eye contact
She moved faster
       until it happened and
       his knees buckled as he
       struggled to stay standing
A devilish smile crept across her face as
       the expression in his eyes softened
       the way the now wet flesh in her grip
       slowly began to

But she wasn't about to stop there

Delighted

We sat at the bar
      waiting for someone to take our order
Speaking of filthy things
Smiling and laughing
      like we were already drunk
Fellow patrons grinning as they overheard us
      talk to each other
      about the plans we each had made
      for one another in secret
I jokingly asked what color panties were
      around her waist
She smirked before pulling her skirt back
      and lifting it

I was delighted to see nothing

Staring for perhaps what may have been too long
      when the bartender startled me
      asking what we would like to drink

The First Daffodil

My finger traced a line from her brow down her
     cheek
     chin and
     neck
Further my fingerprint traveled
Then
     there was the initial touch between
     softly separated skin
A smile on her face blooming like
     the first daffodil of spring

In His Eyes

Sitting so still
>   and trying not to fidget as
>   he moved the pencil across the paper
His eyes seemed to caress hers from
>   the other side of the sketch pad

When finished he let her look

Instantly recognizable as her but
>   the eyes were brighter
>   the smile was somehow warm
>   even in black and white
She had never seen herself like this before
She looked like she was in love
She was beautiful
He hadn't drawn the face she sees every morning
>   when she looks in the mirror

He drew her as he saw her

Colors

It was as if her life thus far had only been
  black and white
  and the way he loved forced her eyes
  to see colors

Difficult Days

She closed the door and
      let her clothes fall to the floor
After turning and spilling backwards onto the bed
      she let frustrated fingers find their way
      into all of the places he'd been

Her mind drifted

This is how she dealt with difficult days

All Mine

We walked down the crowded street
    hand in hand
We looked at each other in silent agreement
    that the time was right
I reached up to grab the zipper hovering
    where her neck and shoulders met

I pulled

Straight down until it rested
    halfway over the cleavage of her backside
She kept walking
Occasionally dropping the fabric that covered her
Showing her skin to those walking in the
    opposite direction
There were many more smiles than scowls
    from the crowd
    as she satiated her appetite for exhibitionism
I loved that so many wanted her
    but she was all mine

Masterpieces

It tickled but
     his hands were warm
The elastic of her lace panties was pulled away
     from her skin
     as he brought them down around her hips
They stayed at her knees
     while he dropped to his behind her
Using his burning grip to spread her ass
     before painting masterpieces with his tongue

Gentle Breezes

The softest kisses somehow led to her skin being
        marked
          bruised and even
          broken in places
Everything started slowly but there was no denying
        he left her body destroyed
Because even a hurricane starts with
        small swells and
        gentle breezes

Heat

Wax dropped and added color to her
      milky white skin
Laying on her right
      a puddle was formed on
      her left hip and
      the candle was set in place
Allowing it to slowly burn
But no matter how close the flame was
      to her skin
It didn't burn the same way as his kisses did
      when they landed there

Faith

The cross hung low from her neck
Resting so near to the bruises
      on and around her breasts
      that happened to
      exhibit themselves so arrogantly
Both worn proudly to display a faith held
      to the savior each represented

Springtime Bloom

Stepping out of the lace brought down from her hips
    her feet fluttered in my direction
    like they were butterfly wings
    and I was a springtime bloom to feed from

Rainbow

Watching her eyes open after an orgasm this heavy
was like seeing a rainbow after a storm

Safe and Warm

There was something about the skill in his hands
    that made her wet
    that made her weak
It was like he was
    molding
    sculpting a new
    smaller version of her

A separate entity that craved depravity

He brought it out of her and made something
    she was terrified of
    feel safe and warm

As long as it was with him

Universe

Her eyes weren't a window to her soul
They let me see an entirely new universe

Self Love

It couldn't wait
She dropped her book to the floor without even
    marking her page

She had no problem looking for it later

She needed to take this moment for herself
    as the center of the polka dotted skirt she wore
    was pulled towards her thighs

Something Salty

Sitting on the floor watching him approach

She blinked and smiled before biting her lip and
    extending a leg toward him
Offering recently removed undergarments
    that hung on the tips of her toes
Accepting them he formed the fabric into a ball
    in his hand before bringing them to his nose
A deep breath in let him know
    she had been wearing them all day

Perfect

He was already in the mood for something salty

Windy Summer Day

Laying there in the light without a stitch
    of clothing to hide anything from my sight

The look in her eyes

The hunger on her lips

A vision like this was
    something you just didn't forget
Something your mind wouldn't let
    slip away

I stepped toward her and noticed the coolness
    of the air and it's effect on her chest
Taking the book from her night stand and
    opening to a random page
    I just started reading aloud
She clutched between her legs
    with both hands as I spoke of a plot
    I knew nothing about

Several times did the sunshine in her hands
    make herself bloom to the sound of my voice
    and whatever was going on in that
    pretty little mind

Each time causing her skin to
      blossom
Goosebumps crawling over her like long grass in a
      meadow
      on a windy summer day

Keep Driving

A smile seemed to crawl across the eyes of
    the face in the rear view mirror

She insisted that he keep driving

It didn't matter where to
    as long as the wheels kept spinning
She demanded he face forward and
    not look behind
He turned the radio off to take in
    the blended sound
    of road noise and her breathing
Diverting his vision from the road
    to her reflection
    let him watch just enough

Her brow wrinkled before an
    indecipherable vocalization
    escaped her lips

Miles on the odometer added up
    one after another

It was painful not to turn around
    as he
    squeezed the uncontrollable hardening
    under the jeans between his legs

Opposite Direction

The steam from her coffee cup took it's time
    to gently meet her face
Reminding me of the pale presence that moved
    from her chin in the opposite direction
    the night before

By His Voice

He was always with her
Even when she read alone on silent days
        the words from the pages
        made images in her mind but
        they were narrated by his voice

Recharging

Coffee in hand
Stepping through the doorway out onto the porch
    of the cabin
Nothing but the summer morning air
    caressed her skin
She stepped with bare feet across the sun faded
    weathered planks to the edge where
    she stared at the suns reflection
Listening as it spoke to her with flashes and flickers
    on the surface of the lake
The growth of plant life recharging themselves
    with the first light of day

She was doing the same

City

The city bustled below
As endless as the waves lapping on the shore
I came up behind her and greeted the skin
      on the back of her neck
      with a peppering of kisses
A clasp was released at the top of her dress
She giggled with approval as I
      pulled the zipper down
Taking so much time
      it could have been forever
Her clothing fell around her ankles
      but she didn't step out of the ring
      surrounding her feet
I stepped back as she turned to face me
Her silhouette was breathtaking as the lights of
      the metropolis below cascaded
      around her exposed skin
She looked like an angel standing in front of
      the gates to the home of God
She smiled that familiar grin
She was absolutely going to bring heaven to me

Let Them

Let them gather
Let them see
Let their eyes light up
      when they watch what you do to me

Treat

One finger sliding across her phone
      another tensely twirling her hair

She was down to nothing but those
      pretty purple panties

Watching videos of other people fucking for
      what felt like hours as she
      waited for me to come home

Stepping through the bedroom doorway
      I was greeted by that
      sexy
      sly
      smile
      and her ass wiggling like a puppies tail
      that had been waiting all day to see me

She got up on all fours as I got closer

My nose could sense what she'd been up to and
      it made me
      twinge
      twitch and
      tense down below

Her eyes breaking contact with mine as my belt was
        unbuckled
Only to look back at me and bite her lip

My good girl wanted a treat

Buckle

Fingers worked to buckle the collar
    around his beautiful kitten

She was so ready

All she longed for was to be
    owned
    led
    cared for and
    cherished

His Sheets

Face down and pinned
       by his weight
Not knowing what to do she
       just let everything go
Crying out with the loss of control

It was so warm

There was so much

For a second all her mind could think of
       was what he thought about her
       soaking his sheets
That was until hot breath filled her ear
       when he sternly whispered
       "Don't you dare fucking stop."

Honoring Her Wishes

Droplets from the bottle collected on the
    inside of his fingers
The sensation of the fluid he coated himself with
    made his desire burn almost unbearably

Her legs stayed together as his surrounded
    her gorgeous ass
He found her and with a slight push
    buried himself
Holding still while she acclimated to this
    new fullness

He began to move

Her hands clenched the sheets as he repeatedly
    and nearly effortlessly
    slid in and out of her
Her gasps turned to moans before assembling the
    words to ask him
    begging him to
    finish inside of her
Honoring her wishes he dropped his head between
    her shoulder blades
    and let everything flow
Kissing the skin below the back of her neck
    as his lips smiled
    and his pulse pounded within her

All Caps

He smiled in print
      kissed in cursive
      and
      FUCKED in all caps

Vino

Some days chianti
Others zinfandel
But always sweet and sparkling
      after thoroughly tasting her

Checkmate

She was the Queen who could take this King
over and over
Making me fall again and again

Across the Table

That smile was killing her
They ate
They drank
And eventually it became painful
        for her to summon the restraint it took
        not to crawl across the table just to kiss him

In Due Time

Kneeling and waiting
      her heart was calm
The silence of the room broken only by her breathing
      and the percussion of a
      slow
      steady pulse

Approaching from behind with outstretched arms
      he made first contact with his fingers
      then his entire hands
Softly swirling around her face like a
      gentle breeze

Taking a small step forward contact was made
      again
She could feel his rigidity with the back of her head

A hunger in her throat compelled her

Several attempts were made to turn and satiate
      this starvation
      but he kept her facing forward

In due time
      my dear
In due time

Well Rounded

She had the eyes of an angel
    the mind of a devil and
    skin that tasted like absolute heaven

Sell My Soul

I didn't sell my soul
I gave it willingly
      to her

Flower Pots

The flower pots had been
      stored away for the winter
      but she wasn't finished with the sun

Song

A melody that only she could hear played to
      an audience of one
It was that song
It was their song
She turned the volume up to a deafening level before
      turning fingertips around herself
Melting to the memories made by the
      music in her ears

In His Sight

Even without any clothing
    she was warmer standing in his sight
Like stepping out of the shadows and into
    sunlight shining in from the nearest window

Pink Petals

It was beautifully painful to watch her
   open pink petals for me
   ever so slowly
I brought my face in close enough
   to smell the springtime
   to taste her nectar
My mind buzzing like a bumblebee that was
   dying to dive into the
   first bloom of the year

Pen

Taking her hand
      he placed the tip of the pen on her skin
Pressing firmly and writing
      "I love you"
      between her right thumb and forefinger
Telling her to kiss these words
      when she thought of him while he was away

Frame

Picking up the empty picture frame
       he turned and held it up to her
She was the only art worthy of
       this amount of appreciation

Entity

Looking over her shoulder as if she thought
      I might not be following
Her eyes said the sexiest things I'd ever felt
It would be impossible to not let her lead me
To not let this entity simply have her way with me

Call to Worship

It was Sunday morning and she heard the
        call to worship
She dropped to her knees and did just that

Intent

He pinned her down and grabbed what was his
with the intent of leaving bruises
but all she could do was smile

Summit

The agony of the lashings grew dull
Still tied and bound
      the pain gave birth to a peace that wasn't
      of the world in which she lived her daily life

She faded from what she knew
      as her senses gave in to one another

The peak had been reached as her
      pulse and breathing returned to normal
      with the anticipation
      of the aftercare he so lovingly gave
Both gave something to arrive at this point

This is where she wanted to be

String of Pearls

A string of pearls is always classic
      and an appropriate accessory added
      to any wardrobe
But I enjoyed them most when they were
      the only thing she was wearing

She Thought Wrong

His grip on the hips above his was almost too much
    almost painful
But the sensation was drowned out by
    nonstop pounding from underneath her
She thought that being on top of him
    was going to give her control
She thought wrong

Staircase

It took everything I had to control myself
      whenever she led the way
      up the stairs
The ache of watching her climb the staircase
      step by step
      was overwhelming
I just wanted to pull her down onto her knees
      before we ever made it to the second floor

Growing

Her arms and legs pointed to the sky
        like limbs and branches
        growing towards the sun
And the smile on her face was the
        bloom of a flower that couldn't wait
        for the sky to water her

Perfection

Those lips weren't poetry
    they weren't prose
They'd be perfection if it was a
    strong enough word

Looking Down

How she adored looking down at his smile
      coated and shimmering
      with her afterglow

Undistracted

A silent room
Her head on his lap
Not a single piece of clothing hid this porcelain skin
      from the eyes that adored her

This is how she preferred to be when in his presence

Fingers making paths through her hair while a hand
      that gently massages is held
      over a breast
Secrets weren't spoken
      they were spilled
Thoughts she'd kept inside for so long flooded
      both of their minds in this
      undistracted moment
Fingertips scratched at her scalp
A grip gently kneaded her flesh but
      most importantly
Ears silently listened as her lungs
      forced her heart to empty itself
      through her lips

Gazing

She watched from above as his hands
    desperately grabbed at her hips

Gazing upon his face slightly saddened her

She knew no matter how still she was afterwards
    he would soften and eventually
    slip from her
She wanted him to stay inside because
    when he wasn't there
    she just felt alone

The Scent

Falling back on the floor
      sitting
      sweating
      trying to catch his breath

She turned and crawled to him

There with her head in his lap
      and the scent of their satiated lust
      in her nose

It was then and there that she could finally breathe

Tucked In

Somehow the moment came for them
     at the same time
Life had been so difficult lately and
     this was exactly what she needed
The kisses he gave to her trembling forehead
The sensation of him spilling and slowly
     growing soft inside her
It warmed her
It calmed her
Like being tucked in after waking from a nightmare

Like a Firefly

She was like a firefly
Caught gently and
     held in a hand that
     made her glow again and again

Conjunction

There didn't need to be a conjunction of the stars
He would connect them all
        as they were gazed upon
Every alignment
Every line drawn between them
        always pointed to her

By Fire

The air was cool and
     the rain was freezing
Nevertheless
     our lips were anything but
Like we were being held together by fire

Follow

I'd follow into Hell
      just to make Heaven with you

Dark Room

She blessed him with the key
      to her dark room
The place holding
      secrets
      thoughts
      feelings and
      fantasies she had felt too much shame
      to let see the light of day

He turned his wrist and released the lock

Opening the door and
      allowing her to spill a heart full of
      what she believed to be darkness into his
An act of vulnerability
Given because she knew he would keep them safe

Always

Broken Mirror

Shards and cracks
She was like a mirror that had been dropped
      laying in pieces on the ground
Even though she could easily cut those who
      handled her
She simply decided to allow time to
      reassemble herself
So others could gaze upon her and see how beautiful
      they themselves were
      because of her

Violet

Under the violet blending of
        a blue and blood moon they spoke
Secrets weren't just told
They were
        savored
        fancied
        elaborated on until souls melted with the
        understanding of the other's
        most hidden thoughts
The desires
        hungers and thirsts that should never be
        hidden or set aside in the shadowy corners
        of the beautiful mind in which they reside
But shared with kindred spirits who seek to find
        comfort in the idiosyncrasies of our hearts
Because what we hide
        if displayed and received respectfully
        could make us all glow just a tiny bit more
Smiling and laughing without the weight of worry

Collector

I am a hoarder
     a collector
Not of items or things
But of thoughts
     emotions
     words I just couldn't say
Even when with those I care about the most

Watch and Wait

I come and
     watch and wait for you here

Hoping you'll visit me to see what's on my mind
Maybe taking the time to enjoy something that's
     just for the two of us to share

Making me feel like I'm not so alone

Thousands of Miles

Those memories still greet me from time to time
The warmth of the winter sun
The blue ocean in which our bodies swam and
       the blue eyes my affection
       couldn't stop drowning in
That red one piece and the way it held contrast
       against her
       lovely
       pale
       winter skin
The smell of salty sea air in my nose and the
       cool taste of
       pineapple and
       rum across our tongues
A paradise surrounded me
       but I couldn't ever really escape
       the stress and
       worry
       that lingered in the thoughts of home
Even when thousands of miles away

Swarm

There was so much rage in the tears she cried
    that
    when they left her cheek
    wings grew from them as they fell

Changing them into bloodthirsty flies

The legion grew and filled the room
Leaving those who entered
    maddened by the decibel of the buzzing
    choking and suffocated by the plague
    storming open mouths and nostrils
    and
    desiccated by the thirst of the swarm

I Knew

The waterfall from the shower head I held
        was so warm
It cascaded down her hair
        pulling it straight and darkening it's color

I sat behind while she soaked in the tub

As I began rinsing the conditioner and
        gently massaging
        her scalp I heard those familiar
        stutter breaths
I couldn't see through the layer of foam that
        suspended itself on the surface of the water
        but I knew what she was doing down there

Little Flower

Come with me little flower
I'll take you somewhere that it's safe to grow

Because of It

Show me every scar
All the tracks tears have left
    after rolling down your cheeks
Every snot-riddled
    sobbing mess
    you have ever been because of the cruelty
    of this world
    and
Let me love you through it
Let me love you because of it

Wishes

Laying in the summer grass
      we pointed out constellations the other
      couldn't see

I wished for her on every one of those fucking stars
      whether they were falling or not

Chosen

There was so much for her to consider
      but
      what he wanted
      seemed so simple
All he wanted was to be chosen

Darkness

There would be no need for light
      in a world without darkness
That was his purpose
To be so bleak
      all she could ever do was shine

Her Favorite Sweater

Arms wrapped around
      locking hand in hand
Her favorite sweater compressed snugly
      around her skin while
      kisses pressed against her neck
No matter how hard the winter
      she couldn't possibly be warmer

Reasons

Visions were surely unfolding behind
       her sleeping eyes
I watched her move and turn
Sometimes mumbling muddled
       incomprehensible syllables with
       those adorable lips
Lips that formed themselves into a slight pout
       that was dissimilar to how she held them
       when awake
I moved in closer
Near enough to watch covered irises flutter
       underneath closed eyelids
Speaking softly I said the sweetest things
       in the hope my whispers would echo
       throughout her dreams
When finished I left a single kiss on her
       sleeping forehead
       to which she exhaled deeply
An innocent breath that somehow reminded me
       of all the reasons I adored her

Path

Every night tiny bits of sleep
       brought the same dream
Over and over I saw myself
       placing stones on the ground
Clarity came after so many of these visions
       wrapped in the silence of the night

I was building a path from my dreams to hers

Gift

Just give me this moment
Wrap all of your skin around mine and
    give me this silent memory
    and the hope that it can feel like this forever

Naturally

She gave all of her body to him
It came naturally after feeling
      how gently he treated her heart

In Between

She could move
      but didn't want to
There were no more ropes or
      chains holding her still
No blindfold taking her sight or
      ball keeping her quiet

There was calm in the restraint and darkness

Being encapsulated by him
      for him
And in those few moments between
      the bliss of her body being used during and
      the peace while her soul was cared for after
There was a time that her pretty little mind
      just didn't know what to do with itself

The in between times

Those were an absence of light
      she didn't think she'd ever be comfortable in
She was so grateful he did what he could
      to keep them from lasting but a few seconds

No Reason

If she wasn't Heaven
       there wouldn't be a reason for him
       to seek salvation

Night to Fall

He sat and watched the afternoon shadows
grow longer and eventually fade
with the arrival of evening
Waiting for the night to fall so he could
be with his love

She Melted

He stopped kissing her for a moment
     to look at her eyes
     and smile

That look melted her

She suddenly wanted to do everything
     she had always
     sworn she would never do

She wanted all of him

She wanted him everywhere

Her hands grabbed his face and pulled them together
     because she didn't want their lips to be apart
     right now
Not even to see the sunshine of his smile

Goosebumps

Standing naked in front of him
      smiling as he approached
Her heart beating naturally as his fingertips
      found their way through her hair
Slowly they slid down soft cheeks
      touching supple lips and
      lifting her chin as high as it would go
Even through palms lifting and caressing her breasts
      the body within his reach remained calm
But when his hands landed on hips
      and
      he leaned in to grip her neck with his teeth
      her skin simply came alive

Control

When she put her hand on his
      it wasn't because he didn't know
      what he was doing
She wanted his hands between her legs
      but wanted to think about
      someone else being there
      to guide and control his touch

Earth Shake

A touch that was nearly painful
    but somehow heartfelt
    held the flesh of her backside

Gripping and releasing to watch
    fingertips leave somewhat circular memories
    on her skin that faded from white to red

His jaw dropped slightly and an amorous sigh
    brushed past his lips as he held her apart
Gazing at the gifts offered to him as they
    glistened from the saliva his tongue had
    just bathed her with

He felt a twitch
    a pulse
    an ache that became constant

Eyes looking down to watch his own flesh
    standing and
    pointing in her direction

Hands continued to hold her open as skin was
    guided to where his head was swaddled
    in her folds like one would wrap themselves
    in a warm blanket on autumn's first
    chilly night

He couldn't stop watching his veins disappear
        as the white knuckle grip he held her with
        pulled their bodies together at an
        agonizingly slow pace
His lungs filling completely before exhaling
        forcefully through his nose
        before moving his hands to her waist
        and making her earth shake

Break Time

Behind on things that needed to be done
Diligently moving from one task to another
       in an effort to get caught up

She appeared out of nowhere

Putting her fingers in my mouth to
       tell me where they had been
I couldn't focus for a second longer
It was obviously time to take a break and
       work on something else

Take Things Further

Four freshly shaven legs found friendship as they
      folded firmly against one another's
      fair skin
The lace between their legs hadn't been removed
They simply held each other close enough
      to feel the heat between them
Looking into each other's eyes

Breathing

Blushing

Each waiting for the other to signal that it was safe
      to take things further

Piano

The illumination of the room was warm
      and I could see her well
With my hand in hers she led me to the piano
      as she took a seat on the bench
      turned and
      took down her top
Her fingers hovered over the ivories as she
      dug through her mind for
      the right piece
She played beautifully from memory

Clearly a virtuoso

I stood behind and watched the muscles
      of her back and arms
      dance underneath her skin

Taking a step toward her and looking
      over her shoulder
      I was delighted with what I saw
Nipples stiffening as her fingers skillfully
      meandered across the keys
      like it was nothing
I caught her eyes reflecting in the gloss finish
      of the instrument
Looking at me in confidence as she never
      missed a note

Ready to show me what else those hands could do

But first she needed to finish the melody her heart
     selected for my ears to hear

Small Moment

Skimming through the pages
      from cover to cover
Looking for just the right words to read
      while touching herself in an effort to
      place herself in the text
Just for this small moment

Euphoria

His kisses following the trail left as the strap
 was pulled over her shoulder
 adding to the euphoria of
 taking the damn thing off in the first place

Christian Girl

She was a good Christian girl
     who gave her soul to Christ
     but sacrificed her body to me

And I blessed her for it

Answered

His every push was like an answered prayer

Crimson Graffiti

Stepping stones of lipstick kisses led
    from chin to chest
Wandering shirtless flesh and building a path
    further down

Delicate fingers wrapped around him
    pulling his skin so tight it almost shined

She then kissed over and over

Pushing so hard she could easily distinguish
    the difference
    between eager tensing and
    the pulse that gave him life
He wanted to be behind those lips so badly
    tears nearly fell from his eyes when
    she denied him

She stroked and stopped before insisting that he
    fuck her hand
He undulated in her grip until the release
    finally happened

She moved her hand once again as he lay back
      to catch his breath
Her touch coating the crimson graffiti that
      she left on him
      with his own lust
Thinking to herself how he reminded her of
      strawberries and cream

Those Words

She had never heard anyone speak those words
He wasn't saying anything out loud
      but she could feel
      everything his tongue had to tell her

His Presence

Slow and shallow were the movements he made
Letting her body become accustomed to the
      silicone lubricant and his presence

Breathing slowly

Exhaling with his every push

He leaned forward to kiss the back of her shoulder
      as the first full penetration occurred
Her teeth latching on to the skin of
      her left arm
An attempt to spread the intensity as
      he stretched her open
Causing colors to cascade behind tightly closed eyes

Owned

These fingers spoke of their intentions in ways
     words could never express
There was a grip on her ass that simply sought
     ownership
And the way her flesh relaxed
     in the pressure of his hands
     was an exchange that silently established
     a new relationship
One between the owner and the owned

Unholy

She looked at me over his shoulder
     as I stepped into the shower with them
Eye contact with me was traded to him
     as she smiled and turned to stand between us
Her arms wrapped around his neck before she
     hopped into his

He held her easily with his muscular frame

I reached under her to guide him in
     after which I joined to her gasps and expletives
Initially the sensation of penetration was
     disguised by the hot water falling
     down her back and onto me
But when we became one the heat turned heavenly

Oh the unholy words that came from her mouth

Cork

A glass of my favorite red left for me to find
The stem standing through someone's
    black lace undergarments

Whose could they possibly be?

So many times I've given chase
    after finding suggestions like these

Not today

I sat and took that first taste of its dark richness and
    let it swell and bloom between my tongue and
    the roof of my mouth
Thinking of her before exhaling through my nose
The glass became empty and there was still
    no sign of her
I poured a second and
    placed the bottle down
She then appeared out of nowhere
    wearing nothing but a smile
Holding her plug in one hand and
    a cork between her teeth

Lace

Her eyes never left mine as she unbuckled my belt
       before greedily dragging
       the pants I wore
       to my ankles

She absolutely devoured me
       and
       I just couldn't move

I had no choice but to let her drain me
       like an insect trapped in spider's lace

Draperies

Standing among the draperies hung around
      the largest window
I gazed at her silhouette like the shadow of the earth
      was passing in front of the moon
Swaying slowly
      the heat of the sun
      magnified by the glass and
      showering her skin with warmth
I approached to offer the heat of my hands
      to the cooler flesh that couldn't bathe
      in the light of our nearest star

Late

Those damn neck kisses were going to
make her late again

Wanderlust

The taste of her skin gave his lips such an
insatiable wanderlust

Pearls

My breath returned and I could no longer stand
       so I took a step away from her before
       dropping to my knees
Each of my thumbs held open a petal to reveal
       the rose-colored gift she had given me
I watched from so close that surely her sacred skin
       could feel my every exhale

One by one

White droplets appeared and fell from
       where they were hiding
Collecting on satin sheets like
       a string of prized pearls

Blade

The cold metal surprised her
      every time it touched her skin
The blade effortlessly cut through each piece
      of her clothing

The panties were last and
      he took his time

Holding still became an exhausting task as
      the knife finished finding its way through
      the last of the fabric
He spread her legs and knelt before her
Tracing the tip of the blade around her vulva
      with just enough pressure to leave a
      faint scratch
Then with two fingers he opened her to reveal
      the bright pink she wore underneath

She felt the cold in a place metal this sharp
      should never be

He held still and just watched as she glistened
      more and more with the tension she held

All before he lay the knife down
        kissed what he held open
        and
        gave her a long lingering lick that let
        the mixture of anxiety and arousal
        trickle across his tongue
After which she fell limp to relax
        and tried to resume normal breathing

Failed

He wanted to hear all about her day
while he feasted on the
open body at his disposal
She tried so hard and failed so beautifully

Bow and Ribbon

Bare feet stepped toward him
Her skin uncovered
Wearing nothing but the bow and ribbon he requested
      to commemorate such a special day
She was the only gift he would settle for

Already Awake

The alarm didn't need to make a sound
      she was already awake
Taken out of unconsciousness by the intensity
      of a dream she dreamed would someday
      be a reality
She turned to him
      landing a firm kiss on a cheek covered with
      beard stubble
He smiled
Eyes closed
      mind somewhere in dreamland
Her hand found it's way and wrapped fingers around
      his soft
      sleepy
      dick
To which his eyelids lifted before he stretched
      and asked if she'd been having good dreams

Pure Torture

Fingers traced her lightly
She tried pushing against him but his touch
      remained soft to the outside of her
      undergarments
Only when she laid quiet and motionless
      did he apply pressure

Pushing and rotating

Feeding the ache within her
It was painful to stay so still
      but to not receive his deliverance
      would be pure torture

Tingle

I couldn't keep my eyes off of her as she sat across
  the table in a booth at our favorite restaurant
Every sip of my drink left me thirsty and
  licking my lips
The topic of our conversation turned from
  our work frustrations
  to things more candid
As drinks were consumed we spoke of the sultry
  things on our minds that stayed quiet until the
  first tingle of intoxication
Her eyes lighting up and
  opening wide as she spoke
I reached out to touch her face only to find my
  thumb somehow in her mouth
Firmly held by teeth as her tongue flicked
  at my fingertip

Someone wanted to be in the good kind of trouble

Fade

Clothes fell to the floor before she turned
      away from him
      falling to her knees
The touch of his hands on her neck reassured
      a weary soul
      that he was going to force the toil
      of her day to fade

Library

The silence in the library absorbed the sound
    of her footsteps
    like a sidewalk covered in fresh snow
She wandered from aisle to aisle
    until

Was it?

It was

Approaching him made her tremor underneath
    her shell of apparent confidence

They spoke

Small talk and banter intertwined
    until subjects naturally became more personal
In a darker corner she took her chance
    placing her hand around his
 There was no resistance
    until he stopped her mid-stride
    taking her hand in his
    pulling her close
    and kissing her

The volumes of literary works placed on shelves
        dreamed of seeing this fire and looked
        within themselves
        for spoilers on how this day would end

But this love had yet to be written

Creation

There was music in his voice and
       art in the way he looked at her
But his touch
His hands
Those were capable of creation

Lifted Him Up

Standing amongst the congregation but there was no
     God in the clouds
     to which she sang
A mortal man had earned the dedication of the notes
     that passed her lips

She lifted him up in song

Singing of the grace he gave to her
     from behind
The forgiveness of sins she felt when he was
     on top of her and
The redemption that warmed her soul when he was
     underneath her
Letting the movement of her hips force him to
     baptize her from within

Morning Routine

It was her morning routine
Making him wake up to lay naked on the table
      conditioned her mindset
      and prepared her for the day
Her warm mug in one hand
      him in the other
She took her coffee black
      while demanding something white from him
Making him weak in the early hours
      gave her strength for those that would follow

Hues

I couldn't help but breathe deeply as
      the rush of it all crawled closer
Her hands were warm and slick from the devotion
      shown to me from behind her lips
I felt the heat building on skin as my
      chest
      cheeks and
      forehead became
      flushed and blush

She was painting me in loving hues
      as her tongue asked and I
      simply couldn't stop myself

The fine bristles making the paint brush
      that was her hand pulled highlights from me
      and they shimmered in the light of the room
After which both brushes were used to
      cover and preserve her art in gloss

Good Morning

The sheets were taken from my sleeping skin
She crawled up and straddled my right leg
      dragging herself across my flesh as I woke
My vision changed from the blurs of sleep
      to the focus of consciousness after
      rubbing my eyes

She smiled down at me

I could feel the room's air getting cooler
      as she left more dampness
      on my leg with each of her movements
I slowly became engorged and upright before fingers
      wrapped around me
Giving my flesh a firm squeeze as if she was
      testing it

She lifted her leg and settled each knee at my hips
Exhaling assertively as she easily slid down

Wrapping me in warmth before saying
      "Good morning"

Spoon

The spoon slowly stirred the sugar in her coffee
      as I whispered from across the table
Speaking in detail about everything I wanted to do
      to that mouth
      to that face
      to that pretty little ass of hers
Eye contact never broken until I
      paused
      licked my lips and
      smiled as my shoe stroked hers
To which she dropped the spoon
      looked around the room and
      brought the cup to her lips in an effort to
      hide her blushing cheeks

Moth

I was drawn in to the glistening on his skin
        like a moth to a flame

Transfixed

I gazed for what seemed like an eternity as she
        moved up and down
        so that I could see the shimmer
        she left behind on his shaft

She raised completely

Standing over an eager cock that
        wasn't quite finished
She knelt beside me and we took turns
        sharing the flavor she left all over him
Bringing my hand to aid my lips
        I barely heard a thing
        before spasms raced across my tongue
I took a breath and swallowed while
        she ran her fingers through my hair

He began to soften so I lifted my head
        placed her smile to mine
        and deeply kissed her while
        our fingernails massaged the other's scalp

So long ago
        but in the days past her sugary tongue has held
        a different sweetness
She is still mine and I often wonder
        if when she's smiling "that" smile
        she's remembering that kiss, too

Bouquet

Ropes wrapped around her and themselves
He smiled as he tied them
Binding her breathtaking body
Adding flowers between the twists of fiber
  and her skin
She was more beautiful than any bloom could
  ever hope to be
Even more so
  as she became bound into being
  the centerpiece of his bouquet

Senses

Bound
Blindfolded
Gagged
      and
Restrained
All was dark but somehow
      she could still feel
      his eyes on her

Joy

Sitting promptly after entering the room
       he waited
She approached without a single thread to
       cover her skin
Standing still in front of him but not allowing
       his hands to lift from
       the arms of the chair

She tried not to smile when she heard a wanton
       swallowing fall down his throat

Turning around and crawling onto the bed
       then waiting
Soaking in the silence before parting her knees and
       spreading her lips for him

She pushed fingers in

Taking joy in each
       pitiful
       desperate breath
       his lungs could find the focus to produce

Trouble

I no longer felt the heat of her mouth
Only her hand moving
     faster
     and
     faster
When I looked down to see her grinning at me
     I knew I was in trouble

Look Down

Deathly afraid of heights trembling hands
    kept a white-knuckle grip on the
    edge of the building

She just couldn't

Alternating between keeping eyes tightly closed
    and turning her head
    to open them and look at me
She watched me with a strange anxiety in her gaze

I could feel the tension in her
    but she loved it
At times nervously giggling when I pushed
    with what may have been terrifying force
    as she clutched on to me

I begged and she finally agreed

Facing forward before lowering her chin
    to the concrete
I couldn't actually see
    but I felt the moment she opened her eyes
She cursed and used the Lord's name in vain
    when they saw the bustling of
    rush hour traffic
    so far down on the street below

That was it for me

I felt the rush overwhelming me and
      fucked her as hard and as fast as I could
      until I felt everything spill into her
      with a violent intensity
All while her insides held on to me for dear life

Beautiful Burning

Fingers slipped through her hair and closed
      slowly as one would when
      catching a firefly
But when they pulled her back toward him
      there was
      a beautiful burning around her head
And shudders were sent
      from where their bodies repeatedly collided
      up her spine to where
      he held on to her so tightly

Together

He was the only one who could break her
      and
      somehow
At the same time
      hold her together

Virtuoso

He was a prodigy
    a virtuoso
Every instrument he used his masterful hands on
      seemed to come alive with music
      that could almost
      rupture a soul
The same was true when he used those hands on her

Homesick

I feel so homesick when I'm not inside of her

Now

Somehow those eyes spoke to me
    while her lips were silent
Asking
    "Please?"
    and demanding
    "Now."
    at the same time

His Own Medicine

Morning's blue light filled the room
        as she sat up and stretched
A groan from her throat had no real purpose but
        it always seemed to help
Her groggy mind trying to wake

A sticky morning tongue swallowed and
        it all came back to her

She could still taste him and the saltiness
        he filled her mouth with when
        he just couldn't take it anymore
She smiled when she remembered his voice
        begging her to slow down
        but she showed no mercy
Adding her hand and making his legs shake to
        give him a taste of his own medicine

More

It sparkled
    shimmered and
    flickered

I couldn't keep my eyes away

Everything was so slick and smooth
    where I was
    but I wanted more
I reached
    gave a twist and a pull that I could feel
    from inside
    as she released the jewel
    and I layed it on her back
Not wasting her sleepily closing invitation
    we parted for mere seconds before I became
    swallowed by her warmth in a different way
She just growled under me
    until I filled her with
    something else that could also reflect the light

At His Weakest

The sheets had grown from cool to warm
      against her cheek
She knew exactly what was going to happen as
      every sound he made echoed in her ears

He was at his weakest

Spilling into her while she smiled and
      savored every sound as he
      struggled to simply breathe through
      what she made him do

Flower Petals

Kisses on her neck
A hand holding to support just under her jaw
Another sliding down the sweet skin of her back
      past a waistband finding flesh to knead

This was relief

A soft springtime sprinkle after a season
      so dry and cold
Surely flower petals would soon grow from this

Marker

There was the tiniest trace of a giggle as the cap
       was taken off of the marker
She spoke of all of
       his favorite
       filthy things
To make sure this canvas was ready to receive ink

Starting her signature proved to be more difficult
       than she had anticipated
The thin flesh moved so easily under the
       tip of the pen

She finished signing her name on skin
       stretched so tight
Adding some X's and O's underneath
Smiling at him when she was done
       to which he merely grinned and
       playfully rolled his eyes
       before looking down and laughing

Doll

Asking to be his toy for the night proved to be
        absolutely intense
Tears welled
        her makeup ruined
The delight in his eyes was undeniable as he watched
        this lovely doll transform into
        the whore he needed her to be
The mixture of their lust dripped from
        both of their bodies
No extremities were safe from
        the freedom she granted
        as he used all of her
        again and again
Her body became his and the release of tension
        from letting go of the chains of expectations
        took her mind to a peaceful place
        it hadn't set foot in for so long
Despite the mess he made of her

Be Still

Not now, kitten
You won't need your eyes for this

Poor Little Thing

She looked up at him helplessly as he finished
making that final tie tight
The poor little thing

Remember

Bruises from the night before
    were simply her skins way of whispering
    "Remember."

Innocence

Hands came together as he prayed for forgiveness
      before even entering the room
Asking a god that had obviously spent so much
      time and heart creating
      the angel in his bed
Asking if Heaven was possible for either of them
      after finishing with the things he planned on
      doing to her

He peeked to find her patiently waiting

This is the first time he had opened his eyes
      during prayer
      and he intended on opening hers even further

This was the end of her innocence

First Class

Her ass was my ticket to Hell
and I intended on traveling first class

Sparkle

A palm covered her
Blessing her with pressure and release
His hand moved away and hers held
      her body open for his eyes to see
A single finger traced her every outline before
      dipping into
      twisting
      turning
      and
      curling inside of her

Pulling back and wandering upwards
      he found her clitoris

Rotating slowly and with just enough pressure
      to make her feel as if she could fall
      into every space between the ridges
      of his fingerprints
Eyes transfixed on how she glistened
      more and more with each path he made
      around her

He decided it was time

Reading her hips' movement and listening
      to the breaths
      that forced their way out of
      desperate lungs
      he let her nerves burst under his fingertip

Barely able to keep herself held open she changed

Ever did she glow
Ever did she shine
Ever did she sparkle

Afternoon Nap

Heads on pillows
A naked afternoon nap
Waking from dreams he reaches over
      to put his hand between her legs
      while kissing the back of her neck
She smiled
      almost snickering when something that
      wasn't a hand
      started touching her from behind

No Need

Acting shy and coy
        she turned away as I playfully tugged
        at the panties around her waist
I smiled and spoke
Telling her she knew as well as I did
        that there was no need for these

Sleeves

Entering the room with a gaze that demanded
    her eyes give his their attention
Slowly swallowing and lightly licking his lips
    to wet them
Eyes stayed locked as his fingers unbuttoned
    the cuffs of white shirt sleeves
    before rolling them up to just below the elbow
The way he always did when he intended on
    getting his hands dirty

Another Sentence

The agitation was apparent to her
It was obvious that he'd had a shitty day

As he showered
      she sat patiently on the edge of the bed
      listening to the water fall from him
      onto the ceramic tile floor

He walked through the door with
      freshly dried skin
She signaled to him and he approached
Leading him to kneel as she slowly laid back
      on the comforter

Knees parted before asking him to
      tell her about his day

He lifted her legs
      placed his mouth on her and
      proceed to tell her everything
She flowed with warm understanding against
      his lips and tongue

She then invited him to lay back and found him
      with oiled hands and massaged his cock
      in a way that wouldn't allow him
      to form another sentence

A Step Forward

The simplicity of his strength was obvious
    as he pushed her down onto bare knees
    before
    slightly spinning her onto her bottom
With ease he pushed the body in his hands
    back against the wall
    pinning her there by the throat
It was bright and sunny
    on the other side of the window
    but the way he threw this body around
    like a leaf in a thunderstorm
    had her soaked
She intently asked for it before
    dropping her jaw
A heart pounding in her chest
    as his belt was unbuckled
    his pants dropped and
    he took a step forward

Training

The heat from her breath caressed my fingers
      as they passed parted lips
She held her mouth open as my fingertips hovered
      above the back of her tongue
Slowly they landed and pushed with
      more and more pressure

She gagged around them sweetly

Tears welled in her gorgeous eyes as they stayed
      locked with mine
Eventually her throat calmed and learned to love
      the presence at it's entrance
The lips I love to kiss slowly closed
      around my knuckles
Now it was time to put something else
      in place of these fingers

Desecrate

There in the house of the Lord tending to a fire
    that couldn't be silenced
On the well trampled carpeting among the pews
        she dropped to her hands and knees
The multi-colored light from sun rays
        breaking through stained glass windows
        made his vision of her seem dreamlike

But this was so very real

She cried out lustfully as he sodomized her right there
        in the sight of the cross
Defying a god who didn't seem to want them to stop
One who was watching from afar
        and
        secretly taking joy in seeing them
        desecrate his home

Epiphany

With her
   every orgasm was an epiphany

Red Ropes

She lie there
     tied and still
Arms outstretched
Sprawled across the bed
     in her Christ-like pose
Red ropes around wrists like
     blood from the nails that
     held him to the cross
She was so much more
My sinner and my savior

Cross

No nails held her to this cross
but she still saved him

Visions

That feeling
Opening the hard bound covers
     of a book you've enjoyed
     every time you let the
     symbols printed on the page
     present your mind with their visions
That's what it was like each time I parted her legs

Harder to Breathe

There were times the fear of suffocation went through
  her mind when giving him her tongue
After finishing
  all was swallowed and
  he pulled back
Somehow
  with an empty mouth
  she found it even harder to breathe

Lightning Strike

She followed through with what they agreed upon
Her arms behind her head
Her legs as far open as possible
The crop caressed her at first
      slowly sliding across the center of her panties
But when it happened
That first slap
It was like a lightning strike
      only
      one she wanted to happen again

Features

I made her stare into the mirror
Asking her to see how
     gorgeous she was
Telling her to describe every beautiful feature
Smacking her bare ass as hard as I could
      every time I didn't think she
      believed what she was saying

Wearing Moonlight

I silently watched her for what seemed like
　　　an eternity
She was so still
Standing naked in view of the stars
　　　wearing moonlight like lingerie
Bathing in blue
Breathing in the humid breeze of an August night
She turned and took a step towards me
　　　and it felt like I couldn't move

I was trapped

Frozen in the summer darkness
I couldn't even breathe until she was close enough to
　　　touch me

In the Night

The kissing became feral as she frantically
    unbuttoned his pants
Shoving her hand past the elastic
    then across skin peppered with the
    slight bristle left after a recent shaving
She grabbed his freshly firmed flesh
    with authority

Moving kisses from his lips
    over a cheek and
    placing her lips on his neck
She licked
    sucked and
    let go before
    sinking her teeth in

He winced and gasped

Feeling his blood curdle and his soul grow dark
Somehow knowing he'd never again
    stand in the warmth
    of the sun
But if he was to be hers
    he would gladly give up the light
    for a life with her in the night

The Cellist

At first her hand moved at a pace that let him know
    she would be taking her time

Adding gentle pressure

Not touching her mouth to him
    she kept her lips parted and refrained from
    swallowing to allow
    saliva to slowly fall

His every ridge and vein shined

Reflecting the light pouring in from windows on this
    particularly
    bright
    sunny day
Gradually and steadily she gave more

Stroking him

Moving like a cellist with a bow in her hand
    putting pressure against the strings

He was her instrument
And when he spilled to mix his fluid with hers
    there was beautiful music coming from
    that man's lungs

Spill

When he caused his own cup to spill
      he always
      whispered her name

Could Ever Be

The time
The waiting
The anticipation
The ache
All were more painful the the lashings
       could ever be

Look At You

Oh darling, look at you
      you're drooling
Let's see what we can do with this

Plastic

It was simply beautiful to see
I held her open as she lay on her side
      pushing the plastic prick in and out of her
I used my thumb to circle her clit until she shook
She then pulled it out completely
      inviting me to taste
I looked to see her grinning as I tried my best
      to suck it clean
After which I soaked it with saliva and
      directed the head to her ass
She shuffled slightly
Gasping under her breath as she made it disappear

August Rain

A hand that could be so loving
      was now firm in the urgency of these
      fleeting seconds
She took a breath after so many of his were
      broken and held as the moment overwhelmed
      and eventually spilled from him
She swore it was summer thunder and August rain
      falling upon her face
Her eyes eventually opened
Focusing on the last drop hanging from him and
      looking at his expression like it was the sun

One Particular Spot

Both arms
Both legs
She had him completely restrained

He lay on the bed in the hotel room she booked
Allowed only to wear the
     blue
     silk boxers that were a gift from her
After standing and
     staring
     for so long he started to speak
     when she stopped him
Taking her panties off and shoving them
     into his mouth

They had been worn for days in preparation

She reached out a finger and tickled a sole
     until what started as giggles
     turned into roars that tried to
     but couldn't quite
     escape the fabric between his teeth

She softly kissed from his foot up his leg

Keeping an eye on those boxers

Watching tiny twitches and jumps become constant
        as he rose fully
His erection lifting the thin fabric that covered him

The center of the raised silk becoming darker as
        she continued kissing
        licking
        biting and
        teasing
The garment becoming nearly black in one
        particular spot as it absorbed his arousal

His thoughts were racing
He ached in his gut
Hoping in his heart that she wouldn't keep
        passing him by
Because he didn't know how much more
        he could take

Jealous

There was a bustle around them
Conversations carried on by other couples
      throughout the restaurant

All he saw was her

He raised a glass while jealous flames
      flickered from the candles between them
Pitifully failing to compete with
      the light in her eyes

Coffee Creamer

The coffee turned cold for the
      only acceptable reason
She didn't use creamer
      but
      oh
      did she make him cream her

Decrescendo

An early morning bliss that was stronger than
the sunrise
All were exhausted as they stayed together after
both of her lovers had finished in each ones
designated place
She held them both inside and enjoyed the
decrescendo of their once
strong erections
At this moment they were her own
holy trinity
After one slipped
she allowed the second to separate as well
They stood and started to clean themselves
before she stopped them
Sending them both
still dripping
to the kitchen to make her a coffee
Because she loved a hot cup after a
good morning fuck

Turning Circles

I watched her turn
    then lift her gorgeous backside
    out of the water
My eyes followed the soap and water as they trickled
    down her legs to join the others
    in the tub below
I wanted to feel the soap on her skin so badly
    but I was told only to watch
I sighed with an ache deep in my soul as I
    watched her fingers move upward
    collect lather
    and
    stop
Putting visible pressure on her tiny ass
She slowly turned circles with the soap and
    I audibly groaned when watching
    her fingernail disappear

Well Deserved

A look
A thought
    maybe more
There's never a time I pass that ass
    and fail to give it some well deserved attention

No Boundaries

Individual toes were blessed with the salutations of
    his lips
    teeth and
    tongue
    sucking
    biting and
    licking between each one
He kissed the top of her foot before lifting to
    taste the sole and work his way past a
    sensitive ankle
    and proceed toward her knee
The relationship between her skin and his mouth
    would have no boundaries tonight

The Very End

Long had she thought about everything
      she'd do to him
      when the time permitted
Now that she had him
Now that he was standing
      tied and bound before her
She couldn't quite decide
So she held her skin against his
      and spoke of the depravity
      she wished to bestow upon him
Feeling the response to each suggestion as she
      named them off
      one by one
Choosing to take her time and save the things
      that made him twitch the most
      for the very end

Offering

A hand cupped underneath as he recuperated
Catching the droplets of his affection
The warmth filled her hand
      a little at a time
      until she was satisfied with
      the puddle that was collected

He sat up and stared at the offering in the hand
      outstretched toward him

She stroked his hair with free fingers and
      told him he was such a good boy while he fed
      on the liquid interlaced with their love

He licked and lapped at their lust until all was gone

Swallowing one last time before laying
      his cheek into her damp palm
      and simply breathing

She spoke again as she lifted his head

Making eye contact and pushing him
      once again onto his back
Letting him know that she wanted more
His voice heard for the first time as her fingers
      wrapped around him and started to move

The Clearing

The path was tread by
    her bare feet
She only paused along the walk
    for seconds at a time
    to remove pieces of clothing
Traveling with the intention of giving all of herself
    to him
    after meeting in the clearing

Early Spring

She had finished me and crawled towards
     my lips for a kiss
The breath she let go of charmed my senses
      like the mixture of lilacs and daffodils
      decorated baskets
      tabletops and
      the air I breathed in the early spring

Precious

They rolled down her cheek
        one after another
Riding the waves of pain and pleasure often
         overflowed down her precious face

I cherished these moments

I knew there had been too many times these eyes
        were flowing with tears from
        a different form of hurt

A pain that wasn't just skin deep

I wanted her to learn how good being pushed to cry
        could feel
To take it all away

Soul On Fire

She was allowed a few minutes
      to rest
      to recover
      before he started again
Showing no mercy
Pushing her to the brink of tears
      but there was no true pain
He alternated between forcing her skin to turn red
      and forcing her to cum
When all was finished and ankles were untied
She closed her eyes and let
      a sigh crawl from exhausted lungs
      before a weak smile tried to push it's way
      onto her face
She was so ready
      and loved how deep she could sleep
      how heavily she could dream
      after he set her soul on fire

Now Show Me

A button undone
Zipper released
She placed her hand on mine and guided me
      down

Leaving my hand without the comfort of hers
      she knelt before me and dragged my jeans
      low to gather in a pile like autumn leaves
      around my ankles

The air of the room cooled my now exposed skin

She came close enough for her breath to
      send sweet swells of heat and humidity
      over me as she breathed in to smell me and
      out to release the air from her lungs

Then she spoke

Letting me hear as much as feel her voice
Telling me to touch myself the way I do
      when no one is around

Writhe

Something came over her as she lifted her hand
     and wrapped her fingers around his neck
She tightened her grip
     tensed her muscles around him and
     demanded he cum inside her
It felt so good to have the power as he struggled
     to catch his breath
While she felt him writhe and spasm
     farther inside than eyes could ever see

Hers to Play With

Scantily clad and approaching him with
      an uncharacteristic assertiveness
She placed hands on his shoulders
        lowering him onto knees that softly knocked
        on the hardwood floor
Picking up the scarf that had so many times
        withheld sight from her own eyes

She smiled while tying it behind his head

Mischievous kisses landed on his face before
        letting him know that
        tonight was going to be different

Tonight he was her little toy

Hers to play with
        however and
        how many times she liked

Expression

Ankles held together
    legs pushed back
My eyes bathing in their two favorite sights
My shining skin sliding in and out of
    anywhere I chose
    and
    the expression on her beautiful face
    when I do so

Drop

Everything was audible from where he sat
  patiently waiting
His mind putting dreamlike images
  to the sounds emanating from the
  other side of the wall
An inevitable silence overtook everything he was
  trying to listen to
A ringing grew in his ears before hearing
  her bare feet taking steps on the
  hardwood floor

She entered the room with a glow about her

A light he hadn't seen in what seemed like forever
His eyes held hers as feminine hands
  ran through his hair
He looked down stopping at her thighs
A tiny tributary of sin trickled toward her knee
Running a finger up a weakened and trembling leg
  he collected what was falling
Bringing it up to her lips and
  insisting she not waste a drop

Therefore

Brightly across a tongue did the taste of herself shine
 as she filled her mouth with him
She gripped his skin with the pressure of her lips
 demanding it follow

He had just fucked her
 and now
 she was finishing him
Taking every eruption down her throat
 as he quaked at her will

Eventually his fullness left as her lips could be
 closer and closer together
 without releasing him
After letting go she slowly crawled
 up his body
 to where her head
 could rest against his chest
Smiling as she knew that
 every heartbeat and
 every breath that pushed
 against the fair skin of her cheek
 was because of and
 therefore
 belonged to her

Asking Me

The air was cool to my naked skin
She sat and watched me step across the floor
      in her direction
Slowly
      just like she asked
I was stopped just out of what would be
      her arms reach
I watched her eyes examine me
      as I stood still with arms at my sides

A wave of her hand signaled that she was
      ready for me to approach

Leaning forward with an outstretched arm
      she stopped me once again
      before taking a handful of my softness and
      dragging me to where she could
      comfortably reach
      while sitting back in her seat

She slowly pulled and twisted my flesh

Asking me to grow for her and requiring that
      I tell her who my hardness belonged to
      when I did

Quietly speaking of what she wanted and
        letting me know exactly
        what she was going to do
        if she didn't get it

Gift Tag

Some gifts were given in boxes wrapped in
ornate paper
ribbons and
bows
But she preferred a simpler kind
Gifts wrapped in cotton and elastic were what
really made her eyes sparkle
And the wetness at the tip
That was like a gift tag with her name on it

An Ocean

When the shell was placed over her ear
     she didn't hear the sound of the sea
She heard the breaths he took while
     buried in her flesh
Forcing her to remember the waves she felt
The small swells inside
     as he emptied and made an ocean of her

Thank you

Grateful is not a word that I use lightly, but it is an appropriate expression of how I feel towards anyone who supports my work. I would like thank all the friends and family who are there for me whenever I need them, especially my mother, Anne. Once again, I would like to thank Alex for the beautiful cover. I would also like to show my appreciation to all of the social media page owners and admins who share my work, repeatedly introducing it to people all over the world.

And to my dearest Sara. This is for you. Thank you for believing in me. It means the world to have you in my corner, always encouraging and reminding me to believe in myself. Thank you for waking up each day and tolerating my all of my ridiculousness.

Printed in Great Britain
by Amazon

37991807R00128